Good Night, Switzerland

TEXTS BY ANITA LEHMANN
ILLUSTRATED BY MATTEA GIANOTTI

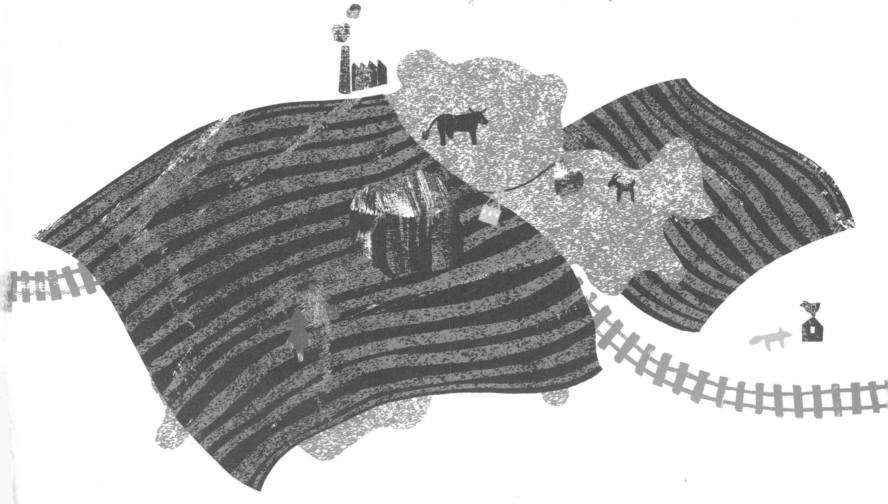

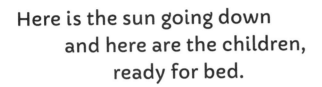

Here is the sun going down
and here are the children,
ready for bed.

Here are the finches, the magpies,
the crows
and here the firs, the beeches,
the oaks,
a playground in the woods
and a hedgehog family.

Cows shaking their bells,
a castle,
a lake with swans gliding by.

Here is a fire with browning bread on a stick,
a factory where chocolates are made
and here is the Aare
looping around
the city of Bern.

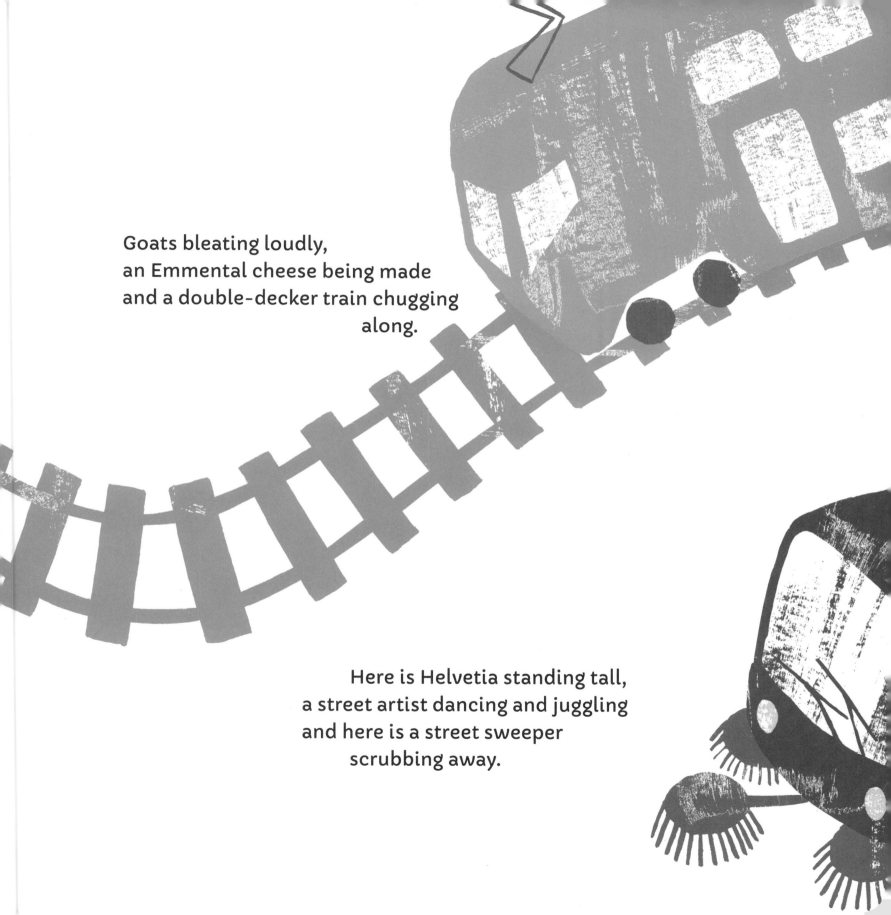

Goats bleating loudly,
an Emmental cheese being made
and a double-decker train chugging
along.

Here is Helvetia standing tall,
a street artist dancing and juggling
and here is a street sweeper
scrubbing away.

A circling golden eagle,
    a Saint Bernard dog,
        the Matterhorn
and marmots looking up.

And here is Owl, wide awake.
    She opens her wings and glides
        into the dusk.

WHO-O-O CHANTS OWL, WEAVING HER SPELL.

GOOD NIGHT, SWITZERLAND, SLEEP WELL.

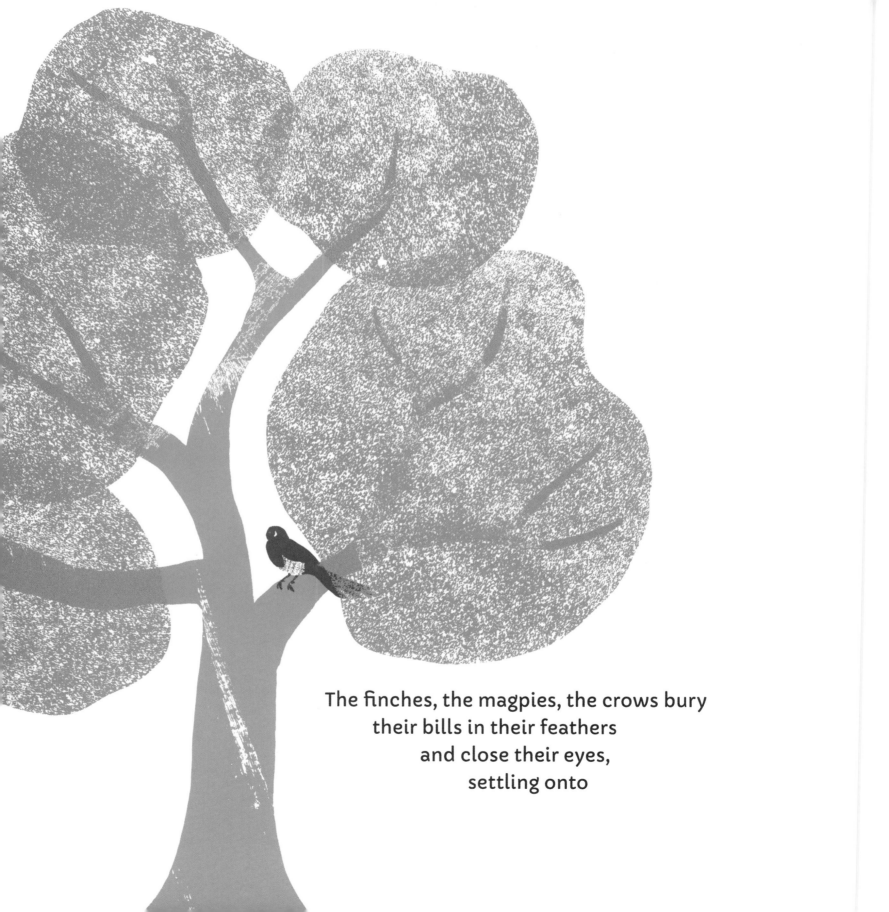

The finches, the magpies, the crows bury
their bills in their feathers
and close their eyes,
settling onto

the firs, the beeches,
the oaks, rooted and
strong,

leaves whispering
amongst themselves,

while the swings sway back and forth,
        back and forth,
        remembering the children
                who played on them today

                and the hedgehog family scuffles about,
        sniffing the air,
    ready for the night.

WHO-O-O CHANTS OWL, WEAVING HER SPELL.
GOOD NIGHT, SWITZERLAND, SLEEP WELL.

The cows quiet their bells,
and lie down to rest,

while the castle walls stand solid and strong,
scarred by memories of battles long gone.

And the lake lies still and inky dark
with the swan tucking his beak under his wing
as he floats off,
water swirling softly.

WHO-O-O CHANTS OWL,
WEAVING HER SPELL.
GOOD NIGHT, SWITZERLAND,
SLEEP WELL.

The fire in the woods flickers once more.
Then embers glow orange,

while the last chocolate drops
down onto a tray,
tasty sweet treat,

and the Aare tickles the stones deep in her bed,
flowing on and on into the shadows.

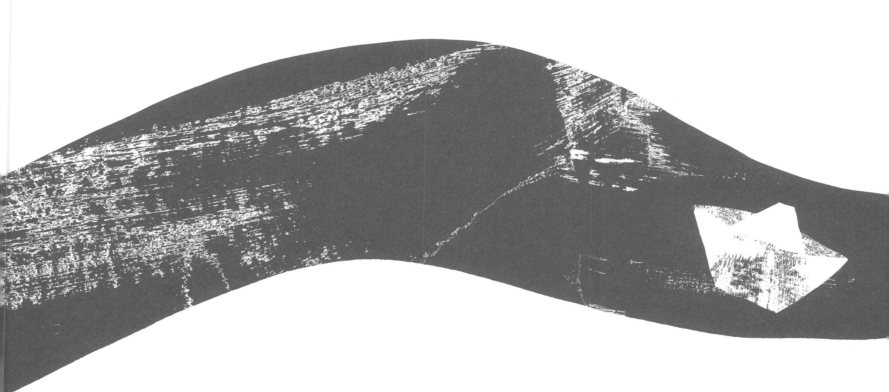

WHO-O-O CHANTS OWL,
WEAVING HER SPELL.

GOOD NIGHT, SWITZERLAND,
SLEEP WELL.

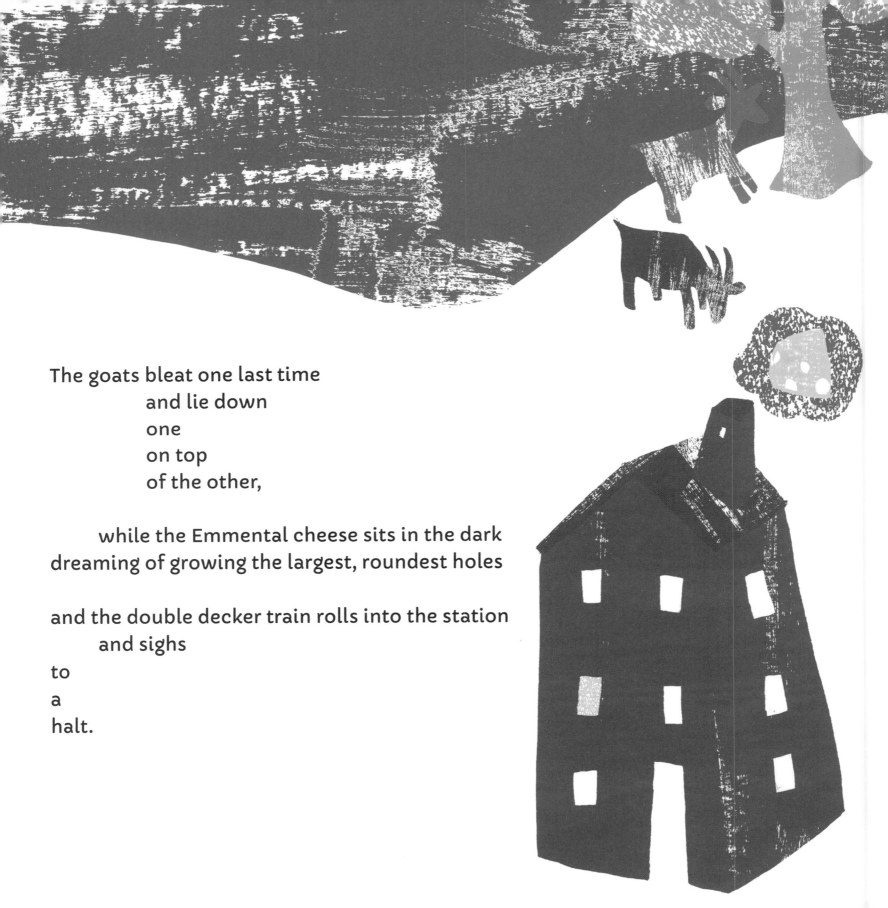

The goats bleat one last time
        and lie down
            one
            on top
            of the other,

        while the Emmental cheese sits in the dark
dreaming of growing the largest, roundest holes

and the double decker train rolls into the station
        and sighs
to
a
halt.

WHO-O-O CHANTS OWL, WEAVING HER SPELL.
GOOD NIGHT, SWITZERLAND, SLEEP WELL.

Helvetia yawns, looks up –
has anyone seen her sleepy?
Returns to her stone self,
always awake,

watching the street artist count the coins
she has earned today,

while the street sweeper shudders
and stops
after a long day of scouring and cleaning the roads.

WHO-O-O CHANTS OWL, WEAVING HER SPELL.

GOOD NIGHT, SWITZERLAND, SLEEP WELL.

The golden eagle locks her claws around a branch,
ruffles her feathers,
and closes her eyes,

while the Saint Bernard dog stretches his paws
and dreams of romping in the snow.

And the Matterhorn blushes deep pink
just as the first stars appear,

with the marmots yawning,
snuggling up warm in their burrow.

WHO-O-O CHANTS OWL, WEAVING HER SPELL.
GOOD NIGHT, SWITZERLAND, SLEEP WELL.

Here is the sun, all but gone,
here are the children
ready to sleep
and here is the blanket covering them.

WHO-O-O CHANTS OWL, WEAVING HER SPELL.
GOOD NIGHT, SWITZERLAND, SLEEP WELL.

ANITA LEHMANN

Anita, born and raised in Switzerland, now lives in Great Britain, where she writes for children and adults. His latest book at Helvetiq, *Slobber Slobber Kiss Kiss*, was nominated for the German Children's Literature Prize 2020 and won the Polish Konkurs *Świat Przyjazny Dziecku* Prize in 2021.

MATTEA GIANOTTI

Mattea grew up in Bergell (Graubünden) and Ticino. She has been working as a freelance graphic designer and illustrator since 2002. Drawing, creative hobbies, cooking, dancing and gardening are her favourite activities. Mattea has previously illustrated *Die kürzesten Geschichten der Welt* for Helvetiq.

Good Night Switzerland

ISBN 978-3-03869-114-3

Texts: Anita Lehmann

Illustrations: Mattea Gianotti

Layout and typesetting: Felix Kindelàn

Editing: Richard Harvell

Proofreading: Karin Waldhauser

First edition: September 2021

Deposit copy in Switzerland: September 2021

Printed in the Czech Republic

Bergli is supported by the Swiss Federal Office of Culture with a
structural contribution for the years 2021-2025.

bergli.ch

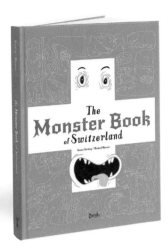

The Monster Book of Switzerland

Switzerland is a monstrous place! Will the terrifying Tatzelwurm eat your pigs and dogs? Can fearless Hannah defeat the dismembered ghost that guards the Aargau treasure? And will Basel's kids be turned to stone?

In eight stories and 36 fact-filled pages, Switzerland's monsters come to life, accompanying readers on a tour of topics that range from how to dig a tunnel through the mountains to what makes Swiss chocolate unique.

By Jeanne Darling and Michael Meister

ISBN 978-3-03869-024-5

Monstrously large format: 270 mm x 370 mm

Age 4 and up

ALSO PUBLISHED BY BERGLI:

50 Amazing Swiss Women: True Stories You Should Know About

This book celebrates the diverse accomplishments, struggles, and strengths of Swiss women. One-page biographies give readers a glimpse into the lives of fifty Swiss women – both historical and contemporary – who inspire and intrigue.

Each biography is paired with a unique, color illustration by Swiss illustrator Mireille Lachausse. Spies, activists, entrepreneurs, entertainers, politicians, athletes, midwives, mothers... Swiss women are daring, ingenious, and brave.
Though the country is small, the heroines are vast!

By Laurie Theurer, Katie Hayoz, Anita Lehmann,
Alnaaze Nathoo and Barbara Nigg
ISBN 978-3-03869-104-4
Age 8 and up